J. R. Brown

Lights on the Way

J. R. Brown

Lights on the Way

ISBN/EAN: 9783337269791

Printed in Europe, USA, Canada, Australia, Japan

Cover: Foto ©Andreas Hilbeck / pixelio.de

More available books at **www.hansebooks.com**

LIGHTS ON THE WAY;

OR

HELPS FOR YOUNG CHRISTIANS.

BY

REV. J. R. BROWN, D.D.

So run that ye may obtain.—1 Cor. IX. 24.

SECOND EDITION.

ST. LOUIS, MO.
ST. LOUIS OBSERVER PRINT.
1885.

TO

CHRISTIANS,

STRIVING FOR A MORE COMPLETE MASTERY

OVER SIN, FOR GREATER LIGHT AND

COMFORT IN THEIR RELIGIOUS

LIFE AND EXPERIENCE,

THIS LITTLE BOOK

IS

AFFECTIONATELY DEDICATED.

PREFACE.

THE value of a book does not depend upon the *amount*, so much as upon *what* it contains. With the majority of persons, the type and appearance of a book have much to do with the reading.

The design of this book is to present, in condensed form, but in good style and easy reading, some of the plain, practical truths necessary for all Christians to have at hand. Books of this class are not very numerous, and are usually in small type and inferior binding, and are soon hid away, while the parlor table is covered with well-bound trash.

First as a young Christian, then as a pastor, the writer felt the need of a book of small cost and safe instruction, to put into the hands of those beset with doubts and temptations. As a help to church members, for the use of pastors and others who may wish to put such a book into the hands of a friend, this work is sent forth, with the confident belief that it will help and strengthen all who will attentively read it.

J. R. B.

CONTENTS.

	PAGE.
FINDING THE WAY	9
STARTING OUT	33
IN THE SHADOWS	61
THE PLEASURES OF SIN	87
THE DOCTRINES	113
LIFE IN THE HYMNS	135

FINDING THE WAY.

O Saviour, I am blind!
Lead thou my way:
Day to my filméd eye is dark—
Even night is only darker day;
Oh! I am blind,
Dear Saviour, I am blind!

O Saviour, I am deaf!
Unstop my ear:
My heart would turn to thy dear voice,
The voice thy sheep alone will hear;
Oh! I am deaf,
Dear Saviour, I am deaf!

O Saviour, I am poor!
Give me to eat:
My hungered heart loathes earthly food,
And heavenly manna craves for meat;
Oh! I am poor,
Dear Saviour, I am poor!

—*S. S. Cutting.*

FINDING THE WAY.

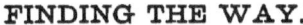

"Come unto me."

"EXCEPT a man be born again, he cannot see the kingdom of God. . . . Marvel not that I said unto thee, Ye must be born again."

Such was the bold and emphatic declaration of the Saviour to Nicodemus, and it comes with equal force to every man and woman. Some great change must, therefore, take place in every person who enters the kingdom of God. This change the Saviour speaks of as a new birth. This change, which turns all who experience it from being enemies of God to friends, which makes them children and heirs, is yet involved in mystery, as it was to Nicodemus. Illustrating this work of the Holy Spirit, the Saviour said, "The wind bloweth where it listeth, and thou hearest the sound thereof, but canst not tell whence it cometh, and whither it goeth; so is every one that is born of the Spirit." The plain meaning of this is, that though the change wrought in the soul of the one who believes in Christ, who is born again, cannot be fully explained or understood, its effect can be. On account of this many who have made a profession of religion and are members of the Church, are much troubled about knowing whether they have really experienced the new birth or not.

There are various causes which tend to produce this state of painful uncertainty. A chief one, no doubt, is the very common one of endeavoring to understand and explain the change itself, forgetting and overlooking the results which are to follow, and which are to be the evidence that it has taken place. The Bible makes it very plain that the new birth is to effect an important change in the character, purposes, and life of all who are subjects of it. The Saviour says, "By their fruits ye shall know them." This means that the results which follow are to prove that the change has taken place.

Another type or illustration of the change is that of entering the strait gate which leadeth unto life. This narrow way of life is put in contrast with the broad way that leadeth to destruction. It would seem that a life in the

narrow way would necessarily be so
different from one in the broad way,
that no one could be mistaken, even
if the manner of being transferred—
changed from the one to the other—
cannot be fully explained. Those who
live in the broad way follow their sinful inclinations and indulge in all
wickedness; they gratify the lustful
passions and delight in sinful pleasures; they may lie, and steal, and be
drunken; indeed, do everything dis-
pleasing to God. The broad way
means unrestrained life in sin. A life
in the narrow way cuts off all these,
and is one of self-denials in following
Christ. It is a restricted life, one
fashioned after Christ as a pattern and
example.

What it is to be unconverted, to be
out of Christ, the servants of sin,

seems to be much easier understood than what it is to be a Christian. This is the condition of all who come into the world. All are born in sin and with a nature so corrupted that the natural course is to sin and rebellion against God. In this state all choose the service of the devil, and prefer it to the service of God. They are "lovers of pleasure more than lovers of God." In this natural state, none love God or regard his law or his commandments; none love his service or his people. To those in this state the Saviour is not precious, and though he died for them, they will not have him to rule over them. All of this, and much more, everybody understands without difficulty, from the single fact that the life they live demonstrates it. It is very clear that all of whom these things can be affirmed have not yet experienced the new birth, and all who die in this condition will never see the kingdom of God.

If, then, the unconverted are of this character, and they are known to be such by the life they live, by what they prefer and do, by what they love and desire, may it not be safely concluded that those who live the opposite life, who love, desire, and prefer to do the opposite things, are Christians, having been born again? In almost everything that pertains to God and his cause, religious purity and life, the Christian life must be about the opposite of the life of the unconverted. Those who have been born again, have been born to a new life, and must be found on the Lord's side and prefer his cause and service to the cause and service of his enemies. The converted person will honor God's law, and his commandments will not be disregarded and violated without penitent sorrow. They will love his service and his cause, and be rejoiced with the sense of reconciliation with God. Thus, in all these things, it becomes manifest that old things have passed away and all things have become new. All of these things, which so distinctly mark the difference in preferences and life, indicate an important change, which, it does seem, ought to be sufficient to enable every one to know whether it has taken place or not. A few things are plain enough: The Christian in his heart must prefer the service of God to the service of the devil. Severe as its requirements are, the Christian would not have the Divine law dif-

ferent from what it is, in its character and requirements. Those who have
experienced this change will be pained
at heart when the Divine will is disregarded by themselves or others, and
they would rejoice to have all the
world in subjection to the will of God.
There are many marks of difference
between those who have been born
again and those who have not; between
the children of God and the children
of the wicked one; but these are sufficient to make the fact known, and to
show, to observers, who are in the
broad way and who are in the narrow.

The agencies through which the
change is wrought that puts the sinner out of harmony with the world,
out of the natural state in which he
was born, and into harmony with
Christ, are worthy of most serious at-

tention. A correct understanding of this important matter will help all to know whether the change has taken place or not.

To all who are lost in sin, Jesus comes as the only Saviour. He came to save the lost, and it was because the world was lost that he came to save it. If men were not already lost there would be no need of a Saviour. Pardon and salvation are offered to all on the simple condition of faith in Jesus as a personal Saviour. The plain declaration is, "He that believeth and is baptized shall be saved; but he that believeth not shall be damned." Much trouble, however, arises to many by not being able to clearly comprehend what is embraced in believing in Jesus as a personal Saviour.

The sinner, by the aid of the Holy

Spirit, the word of truth, or the providences of God, becomes conscious of the solemn fact that he is lost. In this awakened state the inquiry of every one is, "What must I do to be saved?" To this there is but one proper answer: "Believe on the Lord Jesus Christ." The fully awakened soul understands that it must have a Saviour or remain forever lost and suffer the full penalty for sin. In this moment of supreme interest Jesus appears as the only hope, the only refuge. The assurance is that he is the only Saviour; that he is both able and willing to save. Seeing this, the sinner embraces him, lays hold upon him by faith, submits to be saved by him alone, having nothing else to trust or to do. Faith, then, must be simply and only accepting and submitting to

Christ personally; putting the life, the will, and all into subjection to his will, to be guided and governed by him. The sinner who thus submits to Christ is saved, is born again, is in that moment made a new creature and a child of God. In this change, thus effected, the will of the believer becomes subordinated to the will of Christ. This secures harmony of feeling and interest between them, and also reconciliation. Before this all are enemies and aliens, but after it there is agreement. This makes believers everywhere one with Christ and with one another. (John XIV. 20.) This gives a common experience and character to believers the world over. Substantially, they, everywhere, have the same desires, and they work to secure the same ends. They have common sympathies, trials, hopes, fears, and weaknesses; all having and worshiping the same Saviour, his will being the supreme law of all. Thus Christ becomes "all and in all." This necessarily breaks their friendship with the world, and makes them a peculiar people. Believers form a common brotherhood in Christ—one family, hated by the world as it hated Christ. This is very plainly stated by the Saviour when he says, "If the world hate you, ye know that it hated me before it hated you. If ye were of the world, the world would love his own; but because ye are not of the world, but I have chosen you out of the world, therefore the world hateth you."

Such are some of the important results flowing from the change, or new birth, wrought by the Holy Spirit in

all who believe in Christ, who submit their wills to his. Hence it is, that "by their fruits ye shall know them."

In this faith and submission to the Saviour, the believer becomes a partaker of his Spirit. "If any man have not the Spirit of Christ he is none of his." This means that the Saviour and believers are to be like-minded—having a similarity of purpose. This, evidently, is not brought about by any change in the spirit or disposition of the Saviour, but wholly by the change that takes place in the one who believes. All this goes to show the warm and intimate relations which spring up between the converted soul and Christ. It must be plain to all that before the sinner accepted the Saviour and submitted to be saved, no

such identity of will, of sympathy, and interest existed. To be a Christian, therefore, is to be the willing servant of Christ. Christians are servants of their own free will and choice, willingly following the one they. serve, taking him as their pattern and guide. It thus comes to pass that the will of Christ is accepted as the supreme law of all believers. "Thy kingdom come. Thy will be done in earth, as it is in heaven," is a prayer offered by every Christian.

The flesh remaining unchanged, being corrupted and weak, the obedience rendered will not be perfect, and will not give full satisfaction to the believer himself. The Christian, however, will not seek to remedy this by desiring any change in the character or requirements of the Divine law. There will be daily prayer for forgiveness, and an earnest striving to be transformed into a more perfect image and likeness of Christ. And "godly sorrow worketh repentance to salvation not to be repented of: but the sorrow of the world worketh death."

In the life and teachings of the Saviour, all may learn what he desired to do, and to have done, in this world. Those who submit to him and become his followers, will desire to do, and to have done, the same things. Like the Saviour himself, they "will have all men to be saved, and to come unto the knowledge of the truth." This transition, from the old to the new, will interest those who experience it in whatever means are calculated to secure the conversion of others to Christ. Hence Christians are, everywhere, found giving of their time and means to sustain the Church, and to carry the gospel to those destitute of it.

Without anything further on these points, surely all readers can readily determine for themselves whether they have been thus changed in their desires and purposes toward God and his cause. May not all know whether they desire to have done what he does, and are willing to be "laborers together with God" in accomplishing it? May not all know whether the will of Christ is the supreme law to which they sincerely desire their own to be conformed? May not all know, with entire satisfaction, whether they would take pleasure in having all the world in subjection to the will of Christ, and all men obedient sub-

jects of his kingdom? It is, perhaps, not proper to affirm, positively, that any person is a Christian upon a mere profession of faith; but, it can be confidently affirmed that those who have such an experience, and who desire such things, who labor to effect what Christ desires to have done, have been born again. It is certain that the servants of the devil, as are all who have not experienced this change, do not have such a spirit and are not moved by such desires. The unconverted seek their chief good and pleasure in the lusts of the flesh, in the things which belong to the present life. With the Christian the present time, in a great degree, is filled up with cross-bearing and trials, and the future is the time for pleasure and rejoicing. In the eagerness for present gratification many

are deceived and led to regard religion as merely something to enable
those who embrace it to die happy.
There will not, of course, be much
light or comfort in the lives of those
who take this view of it, but there
will be confusion and disappointment.

Why, then, should any one have
trouble in knowing where he stands on
this matter, which is so plain and simple that a little child may understand
it? It is very certain that those who
have not accepted Christ as their Saviour, who have not submitted to him,
are not yet Christians. Those, however, who have accepted Christ, submitted to him, and desire to have his
will done, are Christians. The desires
and efforts of true Christians are to
be in complete submission and obedience to the Saviour; but, with the

present weak and corrupted bodies, the obedience will be imperfect. There will be defects in the lives of the best; but as the purpose and aim of the true Christian is to do the will of Christ, all failures and imperfections will produce sorrow—"repentance toward God." The wicked are not thus disturbed about the things they do, because they are sinful and opposed to the Divine will; but they find their highest pleasure in their sinful ways and prefer them. These facts make the distinction between the two classes so great and marked, that there could be no difficulty in knowing when the change had taken place, if all would look at it in the light in which the Bible presents it. Christianity puts Christ above everything else to the believer. His name, to the regenerated heart, is above every other name. Of course, like Simon the sorcerer, many join the Church who have not submitted to Christ and believed in him, and, like Simon, have neither part nor lot in the matter. Young Christians, therefore, must not make the mistake of taking others for their guide in these things. Those who do this will be led into error. There will be much, it is true, in the lives of many Christians that may be safely imitated; but as none are perfect, there will also be much in the lives of the best that should not be followed. No two persons are alike in their habits and disposition, and they cannot, therefore, have the same experience. Although they are all to have the same spirit, there will be a difference in manifestation. Paul only asked that others follow him so far as he followed Christ.

The Bible is the only infallible rule, and Jesus is the only perfect guide and proper example. Many are too ready to conclude that they cannot understand the Bible so as to be able to follow it. This, however, is because they do not really study it and try to understand it as they do other things. If the word of God were studied, as boys and girls study Arithmetic and Grammar, there would be less complaint about not being able to understand it. Evil ways are natural to all and easy to be understood, and it requires no labor to study them out, just as weeds grow without care in planting and cultivating. Good seed, however, must be carefully planted and properly cultivated.   The mind must set itself to know the truth, the will of God, and earnestly attend to the duties it requires.

"It is thy will; and now anew
Let me my earthly path pursue,
    With one determined aim—
To thee, to consecrate each power,
To thee, to dedicate each hour,
    And glorify thy name.

"It is thy will; I seek no more:
Yet, if I cast toward that bright shore,
    A longing, tearful eye,
It is because, when landed there,
Sin will no more my heart ensnare,
    Nor Satan e'er draw nigh."

STARTING OUT.

MASTER, unto thy feet my gifts I bring,
 Alas! how small;
I follow thee, though far my wanderings
 Ere I left all.

If now thine eye, that seeth all, can see
 A single love
That more than thy sweet love is now to me,
 Oh! Friend above,

Help me to tear the idol from its place!
 For I would fain
Behold the beauty of my Saviour's face,
 And so remain.

I have left all, and so I follow thee;
 Oh! take my hand,
And by the way that seemest best for me,
 Lead to the land

Of light and love, where many mansions are;
 Streams not a ray,
Out through the vista of the gates ajar,
 O'er all my way.

STARTING OUT.

"This is the way, walk ye in it."

"FOLLOW me," is the language of Jesus when calling men to be his disciples. This presents to every one an important duty—following Christ—at the very commencement of the Christian life. The Saviour gives a fuller expression of the idea when he says, "If any man will come after me, let him deny himself, and take up his cross and follow me." Thus, in the very beginning of the new life, all are plainly taught that it requires cross-bearing and self-denials. The apostle says, "The grace of God that bringeth salvation hath appeared to all men, teaching us that, denying un-godliness and wordly lusts, we should live soberly, righteously, and godly, in this present world." Cross-bearing embraces all the burdens, trials, and hardships that may come to those who follow Christ in self-denial and, godly living.

On the very door opening into the way of life is this plain declaration of the apostle: "If any man be in Christ, he is a new creature." This shows, most plainly, that there must be some radical change in all who abandon the service of the world and enter the service of Christ as obedient followers. The apostle, however, assists very much in understanding what this change is and does, by saying, "Old things are passed away; behold all things are become new." This, of course, if true of one must be true of all who become Christians; and there must be some serious mistake when persons make a profession of religion, promise to renounce the world, and yet live just as they did before. A life in the service of the world and a life in the service of the Church cannot be the same, but, in some respects, must be radically unlike. There is one law for all. These facts are clearly made known in the Bible, and they ought to be understood and remembered by all in entering upon the new life. No one can become a new creature, and be turned from the old ways of sin to newness of life in Christ, without it being manifested in words, in actions, and in disposition. Young Christians must remember this, and keep constantly in mind the fact that the world will closely observe the lives of those who profess to be the followers of Christ.

The Bible declares that all have sinned. All who are old enough to know the difference between right and wrong, are fully conscious that they have not always, and in everything, done right. Wrong-doing is sin. Before conversion, all are found living in the ways of sin and disobedience. To be converted, is to be turned from this way of wrong-doing into a new way—into a life of doing right and of serving God. This turning from the ways of sin, which every one must do who becomes a follower of Christ, is what is meant by old things passing away. Engaging in the duties of religion, as all must do who leave the world for Christ, is what is meant by all things becoming new. The direction of the Word of God is, "Seek ye the Lord while he may be found, call ye upon him while he is near; let the wicked forsake his way and the unrighteous man his thoughts; and let him return unto the Lord." This makes the process plain to the most common mind. When Christ is accepted, an open war is at once commenced against wicked ways, and upon unrighteous thoughts. When any believe on Christ, which means to accept and trust him as their own personal Saviour, he forgives them, blots out their transgressions, and inclines them to thoughts and things that are pure and good. This, necessarily, turns them from the old and starts them in a new life. Now, it is in this new way, and new life, that every

Christian has started, and in which
he must continue to the end of life,
if the prize of eternal life is gained.
The Saviour calls this the narrow way
that leadeth unto life, for the reason
that no other way leads to life. He
says it is so narrow that but few
find it! This is a very important
revelation. The fact that it is so narrow that but few find it, is the cause
of serious trouble to many. But all
who have entered the new way, and
commenced the new life; all who have
submitted to Christ and are following
him, are already in the narrow way,
and the difficulty of finding it is already past. Once in the way, the
duties which belong to it are to receive attention rather than the starting. The things that are behind, or
passed by, are to be forgotten, and

those that are before are of first consideration. Starting in the Christian course is but the beginning of a new way of living, and this manner of life is to be kept up until death comes. Many seem to start well, and to run well for a season, but are soon found in their old ways and habits. It cannot, therefore, be too definitely understood, in the very outset, that the beginning is not all. A right beginning is absolutely necessary, but only those who continue to the end shall receive the reward and be saved. The Bible is so full of instruction and warning on this point, that attentive readers will not be misled. Constancy in the service of Christ, and in religious duties, is essential to Christian character, influence, and enjoyment. "He that endureth to the end shall be saved." Those who promise to go and do not, are worse than those who at first refuse, and then repent and go. "When thou vowest a vow unto God, defer not to pay it. . . . Better is it that thou shouldest not vow, than that thou shouldest vow and not pay." See also, Matt. xxi. 28–31.

This necessity for constant fidelity and continuance in Christian duty, earnestly following Christ, cannot be too early nor too deeply impressed upon the minds of young Christians. Religious life is the same in character all the way along that it is at the beginning, and its claims and duties increase rather than diminish. Those who reach heaven must do so through continuance in the way that leads to it, and there is but one way, which way is Christ. He said, "I am the way, the truth, and the life." "If any man will come after me, let him deny himself, and take up his cross, and follow me." This is the narrow way, along which he safely conducts all who submit themselves to him. No one need be deceived, for the ways of the world are not this way.

Starting out in the Christian course implies starting out in quite a number of things. From the hour a profession of religion is made, it is necessary for young Christians to give earnest attention to the things best calculated to strengthen them, and build them up in their principles, and to help them in the way. True consecration to Christ implies and requires the subjection of both the body and mind to him. The body is to be made a living sacrifice, and the whole is to be transformed by the renewing of the mind. The blessed Saviour and the duties of religion must have a prominent place in the mind of the Christian. The direction is, "Whatsoever things are true, whatsoever things are honest, whatsoever things are just, whatsoever things are pure, whatsoever things are lovely, whatsoever things are of good report; if there be any virtue, if there be any praise, think on these things." "For if these things be in you, and abound, they make you that ye shall neither be barren nor unfruitful in the knowledge of our Lord Jesus Christ."

It is with religion as with other things. The boy or girl at school, who does not think about the lessons in Grammar and Arithmetic, will, certainly, not know much about them,

and, as a scholar, will have a very
low grade. The doctor who does not
think of his medicines and patients,
will not accomplish much good in his
calling. The merchant that does not
give his thoughts to his store, goods,
and customers, will be certain to fail.
So it will be with those who start
in the new life, but do not give their
thoughts to the Saviour and keep the
duties of their profession in mind.
They will most certainly fail to have
much spiritual enjoyment, and to maintain a good profession. Religion has
much to do with the mind, and young
Christians must begin at once to give
careful attention to their thoughts.
"As a man thinketh in his heart, so
is he." "Watch thou in all things."

Those who would follow Christ must
be active. They will find much to do.

The religious life requires action as well as thought. Thought leads to action, and one of the first things to be gained in the new way, is to be established in the habit of right thinking—thinking about right things. This necessarily leads to right action. Christian duties enforce their claims so soon as the new life begins. The attempt to live properly and maintain a good profession, while neglecting the thoughts and actions, always proves a failure, and fatal to progress in religious enjoyment. Here, in these things, in the starting out, is where many become involved in troubles which mar the beauty of their religious life and enjoyment. The longer such duties are deferred, the harder the task of beginning becomes, and the more serious the damage every way. This is the secret of the defective lives of many who give much hope in the starting.

Among the duties first to be taken up, and one that is to be kept up to the end, is

PRAYER.

Young Christians will not advance very far in the necessary duties of the new life without prayer. It is in the midst of the most earnest prayer that they are accepted of Christ, and it would be strange if it should cease at once. Praying is considered one of the most difficult and embarrassing duties, especially by those who are just commencing. Delaying, however, does not render it easier, but serious troubles and disadvantages follow its neglect.

This duty is rendered easy by be-

ginning it in private. The habit of
offering daily prayer in private, in
audible words, prepares the way and
makes prayer easy in public, when it
becomes duty to offer it. Christian
duties, be it remembered, are not to
be done merely because they are easy
and agreeable, but because they are
necessary and right. Prayer may
prove a heavy burden to many, especially that which is public, but it
cannot be neglected on this account.
Experience proves that the burden is
made lighter and the task easier,
when taken up at the beginning and
attended to regularly. Any duty neglected is thereby made more difficult.
As a rule, all duties become easier
and more agreeable as they are prac-
ticed and become better understood.
A prayer, to be acceptable to God,

does not require many words nor fair speech. The idea is well expressed in these stanzas:

Prayer is the soul's sincere desire,
   Uttered or unexpressed;
The motion of a hidden fire
   That trembles in the breast.

Prayer is the simplest form of speech
   That infant lips can try;
Prayer the sublimest strains that reach
   The Majesty on high.

Prayer is the Christian's vital breath,
   The Christian's native air:
His watchword at the gates of death—
   He enters heaven with prayer.

O thou, by whom we come to God—
   The Life, the Truth, the Way;
The path of prayer thyself hast trod;
   Lord! teach us how to pray.

BIBLE STUDY.

There is much said about Bible reading, which is well enough, but Bible study is better. The Bible stands first in its claims upon the attention of all Christians. It is the Word of Life, because it contains what is necessary to be known about God, the Saviour, the Holy Spirit, heaven, Satan the great enemy, hell, Christian duty and life. It is the only infallible rule of faith and practice. All, therefore, who are starting in the new life should begin the prayerful study of this Book of books. Without careful attention to the Word of Life, there will be no great advance in the way of life. Many, who do not profess to be religious, read the Bible, but not for the purpose of doing what it teaches, or of learning how to follow the Saviour. They read it because they are afraid not to do so, and having done this much, they quiet their minds and give no heed to its teachings and demands. The Christian must study it in a different manner and for a different purpose; and, having learned its lessons, must reduce them to practice. This should be commenced at the very starting out.

The Bible is the only book that throws a true light upon the way in which the young Christian is starting, or that makes known the manner of walking therein. It, alone, shows what believers are to be, and do, and endure. Young Christians cannot become familiar with these too soon, nor understand them too well. The Psalmist shows his estimate of its value when he says, "Thy word have I hid in mine heart, that I might not sin against thee." "Through thy precepts I get understanding; therefore I hate every false way. Thy word is a lamp unto my feet, and a light unto my path." "Wherewithal shall a young man cleans his way? by taking heed thereto according to thy word."

The Bible is much fuller and clearer now than it was then, and is to be much more to the Christian than it was to the believer of ancient times. The Bible, especially the New Testament, shines with much clearer light, and makes all who study it acquainted with the necessary and practical duties of religion. It addresses all in this manner: "If ye then be risen with Christ, seek those things which are above. . . . Set your affections on things above, not on things on the earth. For ye are dead, and your life is hid with Christ in God. . . . Mortify therefore your members which are upon the earth; fornication, unclean-

ness, inordinate affection. . . . Lie
not one to another, seeing ye have
put off the old man with his deeds;
and have put on the new man. . . .
Forbearing one another, and forgiving
one another, if any man have a quar-
rel against any; even as Christ for-
gave you so also do ye. . . . Let
the peace of God rule in your hearts.
. . . And whatsoever ye do, do it
heartily, as unto the Lord, and not
unto men. . . . But he that doeth
wrong shall receive for the wrong he
hath done; and there is no respect
of persons."

These passages, selected from one
short chapter, show how rich the gospel is in instruction, and how necessary it is for all to be familiar with
it. Neglecting the Bible when starting out is the fatal mistake of multi-

tudes. Many persons seem to think they can learn enough from others, from the sermons they hear, without so much personal study. Those who depend upon these will have a very unsatisfactory experience. There can be no substitute for the Bible itself. It alone "is the power of God unto salvation to every one that believeth." Its truths and teachings are necessary in every situation, and without them no one will have much strength of character, or make much advance in spiritual things. Young Christians who desire to be established in their religious principles, as do all true converts, must study the Word of God for themselves. Its teachings cannot be too firmly fixed in the mind, nor too closely followed in life.

Many neglect the Bible, and excuse

themselves on the ground of want of time. As there is nothing of more importance, all can better afford to provide time for this, than for some things less important. Christians can better afford to be ignorant of many other things, than of the Word of Life. This is the manna—the daily food from heaven—by which spiritual life is to be maintained. Those who, from any cause, do not get the necessary regular supply, will suffer leanness of soul, and be feeble in their religious life. Procrastination in this, as in other things, is dangerous. Earnest Bible study should be commenced by all so soon as they take up the cross to follow Christ. No one will follow him, either closely or well, who does not search the Scriptures to find what service is required. If the wisest and the best need to study it, and be taught by it, how much more those who have just entered the way in which it alone can guide them!

THE LORD'S DAY AND HOUSE.

Bible study cannot be made a substitute for other duties. Preaching of the Word, and the assembling of the members of the church for divine service, ought to be helps in Bible study; and a preacher who has the spirit of his station, will certainly excite a desire in his hearers to know more of the Word of Truth. Those who would "so run that they may obtain," in starting out in the Christian course, must attend upon the services and ordinances of God's house. They should begin at once to share a part in all that belongs to the divine service. This

necessarily requires a due observance
of the Sabbath day. This is the time
provided by divine appointment for the
required Bible study, for regular religious services, and for personal spiritual
improvement. The command is: "Remember the Sabbath day to keep it
holy." This command should be
indelibly impressed upon the mind,
and written upon the palms of the
hands of every young Christian. No
one can become eminent for piety, or
have much religious enjoyment, or gain
any high degree of Christian standing
and influence, who disregards the claims
of the Lord's day. In the very beginning of the new life, the proper
observance of the Sabbath must also
be begun. All who disregard this
command will certainly fall behind in
the Christian race.

The Sabbath, as a season of sacred rest, is afforded expressly for religious purposes; not for personal pleasure, social recreation, and physical exercise, as so many mistake. All the week is given to physical exhaustion, and the Sabbath provides for physical rest and recuperation, and not for social, carnal pleasures. There should be no more recreation on the Sabbath day, or physical exercise, than religion and necessary duties require. The plea for some physical recreation on the Sabbath, such as pleasure walking and driving, is a mistaken one, and without the sanction of the divine law; and, therefore, damaging to the religious life. This one day belongs exclusively to the Lord. The six days are allowed for the pursuit of personal and secular interests, but the seventh is the Sabbath of the Lord thy God. By the divine command it is to be remembered and kept holy. The young Christian, therefore, cannot begin the observance of this day too promptly, nor continue it too steadily.

These duties—prayer, Bible study, and the observance of the Sabbath—constitute the very essence of Christian life. Without them there can be no religious influence or character. Those who are faithful in these essentials, will constantly grow in grace, and in the knowledge of our Lord Jesus Christ. "The path of the just is as the shining light, that shineth more and more unto the perfect day." But this path cannot become bright to those who do not walk in it. The common mistake of multitudes, in starting out, is, in concluding that they may defer giving special attention to such things until they grow stronger, and have more experience. But the only way to advance and gain strength in religious things, is to exercise in the duties of the Christian life. The child has to try to walk, and exercise its limbs, long before it can walk, and it is only by doing this that it ever learns to walk at all. It is much the same way with those who would learn to walk with Christ in the way of life. Begin to discharge, as best you can, all the duties which belong to members of the Church of Christ, and the path will grow brighter, and the burdens lighter, and there will be peace and joy in the Holy Ghost.

IN THE SHADOWS.

Lord, I believe; thy power I own;
  Thy truth I would obey;
I wander comfortless and lone,
  When from thy paths I stray.
Lord, I believe; but gloomy fears
  Sometimes bedim my sight;
I look to thee with prayers and tears,
  And cry for strength and light.

Lord, I believe; yet thou dost know,
  My faith is cold and weak
Pity my frailty, and bestow
  The confidence I seek:
Yes, I believe; and only thou
  Canst give my doubts relief;
Lord, to thy truth my spirit bow,
  Help thou my unbelief.

IN THE SHADOWS.

MANY Christians have troubles and conflicts. They meet with temptations, and do not find the Christian course one of carnal ease and pleasure. Two of the disciples walked with the Saviour to Emmaus, and talked with him, but did not recognize him. They were in great trouble and distress of mind, though Jesus was so near them. The eleven were even frightened when Jesus appeared to them and talked with them. We are inclined to charge the disciples with being slow of faith and blind. It seems that their doubts and troubles arose from their not understanding the Scriptures. Many troubles and temptations come to Christians now from the same source, and there is as great necessity for studying and understanding the Bible now as then. The Word of God is the only infallible guide, and all who undertake to live the new life without knowing and following its teachings, will soon fall into temptations, and find the way environed with difficulties. Jesus is ever near his followers, to help, guide, and deliver them. The Saviour said: "Search the Scriptures"; "they are they which testify of me." This testimony was no clearer, truer, or more necessary then than it is now.

There is no longer a visible appearance of the Saviour. Christians, young and old alike, are to walk by faith, and not by sight. Forgetting this, leads into trouble and darkness. Jesus

said: "It is expedient for you that I go away: for if I go not away, the Comforter will not come unto you; but if I depart, I will send him unto you." The Comforter is the Holy Spirit, which is to reprove the world of sin, of righteousness, and of judgment. The Holy Spirit also enlightens, strengthens, comforts, and guides the Christian. Those, therefore, who think it would be easier to follow Christ, and live the new life, if he could be seen, may understand by this that it would be otherwise. It is very evident that knowing Jesus by sight is not necessary, and would not be so valuable as knowing him in Spirit—being in possession of his Spirit. The unconverted do not have this Spirit, and they do not follow him, but are the servants of sin. "As many as are led by the Spirit of

God, they are the sons of God." Seeing Christ with the natural eye did not make men his disciples, and it would not answer the purpose now, nor diminish the temptations and difficulties of the new life. Having the Spirit, and being led by it, are essential to Christian life, growth, and happiness.

The absolute necessity for studying the Bible has before been insisted upon. This duty cannot be too constantly kept in mind; for one of the most common temptations into which young Christians fall, is neglecting the Bible. Doing this, they form incorrect ideas of their relations to God and to others. This uniformly leads to other serious mistakes, which fill the mind with doubts and darkness. In such a condition there will be but little or no comfort and happiness in religious things. The distress which results from spiritual darkness is, really, a good omen, for the unconverted are not disturbed by their uncertain standing before God. The true Christian always suffers when he has fear about being accepted of God. The enemy is aware of this, and lets no opportunity pass for creating distrust in the minds of the true children of God.

"Pilgrim's Progress" is a most valuable companion book for the Bible. It throws much light upon the Christian's way, and illustrates many of the things that throw shadows on the path and give trouble. The Christian way and life are new to all who enter upon them, whether young or old. Very few advance far, before, like Pilgrim, they are beset with difficulties, and troubled with doubts. They forget that many old habits and associations must be abandoned, and new ones formed. This constitutes a very large and important part of the new, or Christian life. This separation from old ways will not be satisfactorily accomplished without a fixed purpose, and constant fidelity to the duties of the way. There are many ways, but only one right way; only one that leads to heaven, while there are many leading to destruction. Some of these false ways run so nearly with the true one that multitudes are deceived and conclude they are so near the right, and so little wrong, that they need not give themselves trouble about it. The great enemy is wise and seeks to deceive and lead astray, and he cares but little what way one is in so it is not the right one, or how near one may

be to the right way, so not actually in it.

Many are deceived and brought into darkness, with the idea that the Christian life is to be one of uninterrupted ease and pleasure; and, when disappointments, temptations, and sorrows arise, they are ready to despond. The Bible, however, guards all against such error, and those who know it best, and follow its instructions most diligently, will succeed best and have the most religious enjoyment, and be troubled with fewest doubts. Pilgrim encountered the Hill Difficulty and the lions, and got out of his way because he did not follow the instructions of his Roll. So it is with all who neglect the Bible.

The new birth, or the change wrought in the person who renounces the world and believes in Christ, is a spiritual change, not physical. The body is not born again, as Nicodemus thought it must be when the Saviour was telling him of the change that must take place in order to be saved. Regeneration is spoken of as the renewing of the mind, not of the body. The body remains the same after as before the change, hence it does not make the person perfect, or free from tendencies to do wrong by gratifying the carnal appetites and passions. Remembering this will help all to understand much that would otherwise be mysterious and cause trouble.

The body is the seat of carnal desires and appetites, which cannot be gratified without the mind being filled with trouble and fears. It should be constantly kept in mind that these

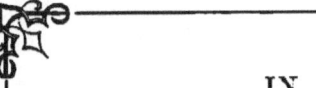

evil tendencies of the body must be vigilantly watched and guarded against. No one can advance in the new life, or take pleasure in religious experience, exercises, and duties without this.

The body not being renewed with the soul, in conversion, there is found in every Christian an influence not in harmony with the renewed mind. The body, with its tendencies to evil, is to be brought into subjection to, and controlled by, the renewed soul. The Christian, therefore, finds a conflict within himself. The Apostle Paul describes this condition when he says: "That which I do, I allow not: for what I would, that do I not; but what I hate, that do I." "Now then it is no more I that do it, but sin that dwelleth in me. For I know that in me (that is, in my flesh)

dwelleth no good thing: for to will is present with me; but how to perform that which is good I find not." "I find then a law, that, when I would do good, evil is present with me. For I delight in the law of God after the inward man: but I see another law in my members, warring against the law of my mind, and bringing me into captivity to the law of sin which is in my members." "So then with the mind I serve the law of God; but with the flesh the law of sin." "We are debtors, not to the flesh, to live after the flesh. For if ye live after the flesh, ye shall die: but if ye through the Spirit do mortify the deeds of the body ye shall live." "I keep under my body and bring it into subjection."

No change is wrought in any of

the natural senses of the body by the work of regeneration. Liquor will taste the same, and produce drunkenness after conversion the same as before, and those who would not be overtaken by this sin must not drink liquor. A person may have the same kind of pleasure from the gratification of the fleshly appetites and passions, after conversion as before. This leads multitudes into most serious trouble. These are "the pleasures of sin." Many things may give real pleasure and gratification, and yet be very wrong, and produce darkness and sorrow of heart. The Christian life is not all pleasure, nor is all pleasure sinful. The devil, being crafty, takes advantage of all these facts and deceives many, hinders their progress, and obscures the light of their lives.

In the resurrection the body will be purified and all evil tendencies taken away, and there will then be entire harmony between the body and soul. This subject has been mentioned here for the purpose of calling attention to the body as a source of trouble to the Christian, and of guarding all against yielding to the demands of carnal desires. Many think that it is right to do whatever they are inclined to do, but this is a mistake. The inclinations of the renewed soul, it is true, are to that which is right, but those of the unrenewed body are to evil. This should be kept in mind, so that the evil may be guarded against and the good followed.

Of the many things leading the young Christian into doubt and trouble that may be here mentioned, are:

1. Ignorance of duty. This is partly unavoidable, for our knowledge is not perfect in this life. · Do the best we can, there will be much that the wisest will not know. When we get out of the way, or, from any cause, fail to do our duty, there will be loss of spiritual light and enjoyment. The chief trouble, however, arises from ignorance that might be avoided by a proper attention to the Word of God and the claims of religion upon the present life. Christians are disciples, which means that they are learners and that they must give due attention to the things to be learned from the teachings of Christ. Those who start in the new way should begin at once to learn all they can of the claims and obligations of their new calling. The ignorance which

comes from the want of effort to be informed is a much more serious affair. Those who have means and opportunities for learning their duty, but do not improve them, cannot escape the evil consequences on the ground of ignorance. The Saviour said: "That servant, which knew his lord's will, and prepared not himself, neither did according to his will, shall be beaten with many stripes. But he that knew not, and did commit things worthy of stripes, shall be beaten with few stripes. For unto whomsoever much is given, of him shall be much required; and to whom men have committed much, of him they will ask the more." Before the Bible was printed but few .could have a copy of it, and might be excused for even great lack of knowledge, but now every Christian can have a copy and is without excuse. Then, many might be ignorant of much of its teachings, but now all can study and understand it. Those who would now escape the evils of not knowing the Bible must study it—must study to show themselves approved unto God.

2. Neglect of known duties is the greater and more common source of trouble to all who enter the service of Christ. The influences leading to this are numerous. All know better than they do; and, as a consequence, all have more or less of darkness and trouble in their Christian life and experience. One error leads to another; the neglect of one duty leads to the neglect of another, and in this way the trouble augments itself in a fearful ratio.

Many are misled by the fact that duties sometimes seem so hard, uninteresting, and difficult, and on this account they are not taken up. They conclude that duty to the Christian should be always agreeable, and easily performed; but the Bible and all experience show that this is an error. Were the body renewed in conversion, the conquest would be easy; but, as it is not, a complete victory can be gained only by earnest attention and effort, and a constant looking to Christ. It is a great victory when gained, but is to be reached through faithful exercise in the duties required. Those who are unwilling to endure this hardness as good soldiers, will not have a satisfactory life. Those, then, who would avoid trouble, doubt, and darkness, must be faithful and constant in

duty, whether it be easy and agreeable
or not. Only in this way can they
walk in the light of God, and rejoice
in all their sorrows and trials.

3. A fruitful source of trouble and
deadness, with many who become church
members, is improper company. There
is, perhaps, nothing more dangerous to
young Christians. It may be very
difficult, in many instances, to break
away from old associations, but it must
be done. It is common to overlook
the teachings of the Bible on this
point, yet they are very plain. The
book of Psalms opens with these sig-
nificant words: "Blessed is the man
that walketh not in the counsel of
the ungodly, nor standeth in the way
of sinners, nor sitteth in the seat of
the scornful." Paul says: "Be ye not
unequally yoked together with unbe-

lievers: for what fellowship hath righteousness with unrighteousness? and what communion hath light with darkness? and what concord hath Christ with Belial? or what part hath he that believeth with an infidel? and what agreement hath the temple of God with idols? for ye are the temple of the living God; as God hath said, I will dwell in them, and walk in them; and I will be their God, and they shall be my people. Wherefore come out from among them, and be ye separate, saith the Lord." Speaking directly upon this subject, Solomon says: "Can a man take fire in his bosom and his clothes not be burned? Can one go upon hot coals and his feet not be burned?" The thoughts, language, and practices of the irreligious, as a rule, are so unlike

those of the Christian, that the two
cannot be intimately associated without
injury to the latter. All, therefore,
who desire to maintain a good profession, must pay due attention to the
character of those whom they select
for companions. Those who do not do
this. will most certainly have trouble,
doubts. and darkness.

4. The neglect of prayer and communion with God is a most common
cause of difficulty. When the Christian
prays he is in communion with God,
and those who are regular and earnest
in this duty. will not get far out of the
way. Prayer puts and keeps the
Christian in the position to receive the
blessings and comforts God has for all
true worshipers. Those who neglect
this duty will not only be deprived of
the good it brings, but also suffer cold-

ness and leanness of soul. In this
way the believer is weakened, and
robbed of the purest joys.

5. Conforming to the world in its
practices, fashions, and pleasures.
There is an essential difference between
the Church and the world. This difference begins at conversion, and is to
increase with the years. Those who
become disciples and followers of Christ,
must ever remember that the world is
not to be their guide. The world, the
flesh, and the devil, are the three great
enemies to the Christian, and they must
be resisted and overcome. This cannot
be done by yielding to them, or following after them. Those, then, who would
enjoy the comforts of religion, and
maintain a good profession, must not
be conformed to the world.

6. Failing to make honest confession

to God of wrong done, or of duty neglected, brings trouble to all who do it. The child that hides its mistakes and wrong-doings from its parents, will not be happy; and, most likely, will be led into greater wrongs. It is the same with the Christian who fails to make acknowledgment to God; for, "If we confess our sins, he is faithful and just to forgive us our sins, and to cleanse us from all unrighteousness." This should form a part of daily prayer, and those who honestly follow it will be richly rewarded in the peace of mind that will result from it. But to be of value, such confessions must be followed by reformation, and by earnest efforts to avoid a repetition of the wrong. The prayer of the Psalmist was: "Cleanse thou me from secret faults." The sins committed in secret are, perhaps, more dangerous than those committed openly, for the reason that they are more likely to be covered up. But God knows the heart and all secret sins, and it is best and safest to be honest with him.

7. There is, perhaps, no more prolific source of trouble to the Christian than evil thoughts. "As a man thinketh in his heart, so is he." The Christian must keep a constant watch over his thoughts, for without this there will be little comfort or advance in religious things. Evil thoughts are so insidious, that they corrupt the life almost unconsciously. There must be constant attention to the matter of keeping the thoughts pure; and to be pure, they must be upon proper objects. All who would live a true and consistent Christian life, must strive to keep the mind from impure things, and upon such as

are pure. The danger is great, and the necessity for faithfulness in watching is also great. So long as the devil can keep the mind as a cage of unclean birds, and the thoughts, especially in secret, upon improper things, he will have the person in his power.

There are other sources of trouble to the Christian, but if what have been named receive due attention, there will not be much difficulty in escaping from others. Neglect of these will blight any life, and those who desire to walk in the light and to enjoy religion, must give attention to them. The evils which arise from the neglect of Christian duties, do not fall upon the unfaithful ones only, but also upon those who are more faithful, and upon the Church and cause. When one member suffers, the whole body suffers with it. The trials

of one member of a family affect and
involve all the members. In all these
Christ is the help and light of those
who sincerely desire to serve him and
honor their calling.

"Oft my path is dark and drear,
And my heart is filled with fear,
Yet I hear my Saviour's voice,
And his words my heart rejoice.

When the fearful tempest blows,
When my enemies oppose,
While the storm is passing by,
Still I hear my Saviour nigh.

When I tread death's gloomy vale,
Still his presence shall not fail;
Then his staff will be my stay,
And I'll hear my Saviour say:

I will guide thee, I will guide thee,
In the way I will instruct thee."

THE PLEASURES OF SIN.

"Lord, I will follow thee," I said,
  "And give to thee my heart;
And for the world and self will keep
  Only a little part;
A little part, what time my soul
  Grows weary, worn, and sad,
A little spot where earthly joys
  May come to make me glad."
But on my ear, it seemed to me,
  I heard a whisper fall:
"I cannot halve thy heart with thee;
  Give none to me—or all."

"But, Lord, the world is fair," I said,
  "I would not go astray,
Yet sometimes may I pluck a flower
  Outside the narrow way?
Yet sometimes may I sit serene,
  Nor spirit-conflicts share,
Just shifting for a space, the Cross
  I am content to bear?"
Yet once again, it seemed to me,
  I heard the whisper fall:
"I cannot halve thy heart with thee;
  Give none to me—or all."

THE PLEASURES OF SIN.

THE present life is not a play-time. It is a brief season afforded for earnest engagement in the most important duties. In the time allotted, the eternal happiness or misery of every soul is to be determined. The claimed necessity for so much time to be spent in self-indulgence and carnal gratification, is greatly magnified. Many more are injured by idleness and excessive pleasure, than by over attention to necessary duties. More souls are ruined by not beginning early enough, than by embracing religion too soon. Christians, no doubt, need some relaxation from the sterner duties which every day demand attention. But, in whatever this recreation may be, it must not be such as will destroy Christian character and influence.

With all who are true Christians, the duty of maintaining correct religious principles and habits of life, must be of pre-eminent importance. The true church member cannot place any temporary pleasure or carnal gratification above Christian fidelity and example. Whatever of self-denials, trials, and reproaches may come to the Christian, in whatever business or situation he may be placed, the profession he has made must be held fast.

So certainly as there is such a thing as a new life—a life in Christ—must there be a difference between the pleasures and pursuits of those who live this life, and those who do not. Too

many, however, do not fully comprehend
this truth, because they entertain the too
common idea that it does not apply to
young Christians. This is a most
serious mistake; one that leads to
much trouble, and has made shipwreck
of multitudes. The world, however, has
no trouble on account of questionable
pleasures and amusements. The broad
way is wide enough to take in the dance,
the theatre, the card-table, the wine-
cup—in short, every form of pleasure
and carnal gratification which a common
depravity covets. The world has no
qualms of conscience, or questions of
liberty or propriety, about a religious
character and life, and is, therefore, not
troubled as are they who are not of this
world, as the Saviour · declared his
followers to be. The world throngs the
broad way, but the way of the Christian,

however young, is narrow, and sets a strict limit to the things which are to be allowed to those who are in it. This way is declared so narrow by the Saviour himself, that but few find it.

All true Christians, young and old, are in this narrow way, and in it they are to find all of the privileges and pleasures which the Bible allows, and which a life of self-denial in following Christ affords them. Only those who walk in this way, can be the light of the world and the salt of the earth, which the Saviour says his true followers are. When Christians forget this, and conform to the world—go with the world in the broad way—and seek pleasure and amusement in things that are purely worldly and sensual, they lose the higher pleasures of religion; and the light that should be in them to lead the world to a higher and better life, becomes darkness. There is no power, light or influence, in either the dance, the theatre, the wine-cup; in billiards, cards, or the race-course, to make any person lead a better life. There is nothing in any or all of these, to lead any soul out of sin into newness of life; to draw any one from the way of death into the way of life. Practices or pleasures so wholly void of any moral or purifying influences, or impulses, and which so uniformly and completely dwarf the religious life, and which rob those who indulge in them of their influence and enjoyment, cannot possibly afford proper amusement or recreation for the children of God, either young or old.

No one was ever saved from sin, or reformed in life, by church members dancing, playing cards and billiards, going to the theatre, or by drinking liquor; but multitudes, by them, are influenced to evil, and led to dissipation, to crime, and to hell!

In the eager pursuit of present pleasures, it is very easy to forget that the present life is to be one of sacrifices and self-denials to those who follow Christ. This is so, for the reason that it is better for both Christians and for others. Upon being received into the Church, members publicly accept Christ as their pattern and guide. In this they take the vow of separation from the world. This has its restraining influence upon the pleasures of sin, as truly as upon other things that are sinful. The promised reward of an eternal life of unalloyed pleasure is future, and is to be entered upon after the trials and self-denials of the present life are ended. The self-denials of following Christ embrace many things that would afford Christians the same kind of pleasures they do the irreligious. Such things are to be avoided; not because there is no pleasure in them, but because the pleasure is sinful, and destroys Christian character and influence. These things cannot be too well understood, and too constantly remembered by all young Christians. They need to watch, and to be on their guard against the temptations and snares of the enemy. The exhortation is, to "watch and be sober."

Present and carnal pleasure, preferred to self-denial and following Christ, leads to certain endless misery. This is as true of the young as of the old, and young Christians must resist the temptation to sinful indulgence, and avoid it as truly as must the old.

These things show the difference between the two classes—between those who are true church members and those who are not—to be almost infinite. The difference, however, in both character and pursuits, is no greater than God himself has made it, and revealed it in his Word. This difference, in character and life, in desires and purposes, however great, must exist here, and be maintained during this present life, and be made manifest in the pleasures and pursuits of the present time. It is as absolutely necessary to maintain religious character and deportment in pleasures and recreations, as in business and acts of worship. The difference between the Church and the world must be as marked, and well defined in social

amusements, as in any of the walks of
life. There is, indeed, greater need of
vigilance in the things which the enemy
presents as so nearly harmless, and so
congenial to the natural desires and
feelings. By these illusive pleasures of
sin, more church members are deceived
and their influence and happiness destroyed, than by business, or the greater
sins of theft, adultery, murder, etc.

This view of the Christian course by
no means makes religion "pale and
bilious," gloomy and repulsive, as some
are so ready to represent it. It does
not make the Christian life any more
cheerless than the Saviour himself made
it, and presents it to all who accept it
of him. The Saviour was as earnest in
warning his followers against being
conformed to the world in the pleasures
of sin, as against what are generally

regarded as the greater sins and vices
of society. The Christian finds in the
duties of religion, which are consistent
with his profession of the renunciation
of the world, in avoiding "the appearance of evil," pleasures inexpressibly
purer and higher—joys which the world
has not, and which it can "neither give
nor take away." These grow in num-
bers and intensity with the advance in
the Christian life, but those of the
world decrease as age comes on. There
is absolutely no *Christian* pleasure or
enjoyment in either the dance, the
theatre, card-playing, or the wine-cup;
but, sooner or later, there is sorrow
and anguish to every one who indulges
in them. No one need be deceived in
this particular, for to all who are not set
to do evil, the evidence is overwhelm-
ing. Indulgence in these things yields

nothing good. No member of the Church, young or old, can engage in them without loss of religious influence and enjoyment, and personal self-respect, more valuable than all worldly pleasures. There is no good in them anywhere, or upon any occasion. There is no safety from their evil influence, but in total abstinence.

It is a first duty of parents and religious teachers to inform and guard their children and young Christians against temptations which appear in the garb of innocence, as do all of the pleasures of sin. It is of the utmost importance to young Christians themselves, and also to the cause of Christ, that they establish and maintain a proper religious character while young. Starting right is as important and necessary in the religious life as in business life. Those

who start wrong in the Christian course, will be a thousand times more likely to continue and end in error. This will leave them but little pleasure and peace of mind, and will rob them of their Christian influence, destroy their usefulness, and in their last hours, if not before, will bring darkness and sorrow.

It does not come within the design of this little book to speak in detail of the character of these amusements. They are to be known by what they produce in those who indulge in them —"by their fruits ye shall know them." Take all those named, the theatre, dance, card-playing, billiards, and the wine-cup, and, almost without exception, the voice of the Christian world is against them. General Assemblies, Conferences, and the various courts of all Churches, have condemned them, and declared their influence to be such that Christians cannot indulge in them without damage to their own standing, and to the cause of religion. Such facts ought to have great weight upon all, for the unanimous voice of the Churches is more likely to be right, than the opinions of individuals seeking gratification. It is well known that the church members who are the most worldly in their lives, and the least like Christ, encourage these amusements, and indulge in them most. The most earnest, devoted, and successful Christian workers, old and young, in all Churches, believe them evil in their influence, and do not engage in them, nor encourage others to do so. There is a reason for this, and it must be obvious to all who are not blinded by the desire to engage in them, or in some way to be profited by them. All experience shows that indulgence in these things, weakens the religious interest, and dwarfs the spiritual life and enjoyment. No true Christian can be found who believes there is any spiritual exercise or benefit in these pleasures of the world, but multitudes of men and women are led to disgrace and ruin by them. Millions of the best men and women, of this and other ages, unite in declaring them evil, and only evil, in their influence, and to be shunned by all who would honor God by a consistent Christian life.

It must be the desire and purpose of true Christians to maintain a good profession before the world. The covenant embraces their example and personal influence, by which they will seek to help and persuade others to a better

life. But this will not be the reward
of those church members found in the
ball-room and theatre, or with cards or
the wine-cup in their hands. They run
into temptation, and lead others with
them, and both suffer together. There is
absolute safety in keeping out of temptation, but to do this, the places where
these things are done must be shunned.
It is absolutely certain that those who
are never found where these things are
done, will never be tempted and overcome by them. This is safety, and all
can have it who sincerely desire it.
The probability is, that those who
habitually go where these things are
done, will yield to the temptation.

It is, perhaps, impossible for all
Christians to always avoid such occa-
sions and places; but when this is so,
they must have the courage to refuse

to join in them, as they will always be urged to do. Those church members who are most under the influence of the world, will, as a rule, importune others to join them. Christians must have some self-respect, and be independent enough to say no, when asked to do anything that will compromise them with the world. God does not require any one to sacrifice character and self-respect, but the devil does. Those who think less of Christians for refusing to do anything that will in any degree damage their character or the cause of Christ, are neither true friends nor proper associates. Those who do wrong, will lose the respect of those who induce them to do it. The wicked respect most those who respect themselves, and stand by their principles.

Those who never indulge in these
things, will neither be injured by them,
nor lead others into them. Those who
are led away and destroyed by these
sinful amusements, and who lead others
into them, are those who learn them
and indulge in them. Safety in all of
these things, is found in keeping out
of the way of temptation, and in
refusing to be led into it by others.
Christians, young and old, have every
thing to gain by standing to their
principles, and maintaining their integ-
rity, and they lose everything by
abandoning them for any earthly
consideration.

Young people influence each other
much more than do those of maturer
years. They are freer in their inter-
course, and more impulsive, and they
are more apt to follow each other.

Young church members ought to have
influence over their young associates,
and find delight in winning them to a
better life. This they cannot do by
joining them in their sinful practices
and pleasures, but by showing them
that religion gives something that is
higher and better. Many are deceived
by the idea that by joining others in
their evil practices, they can win them
to a better way. This is doing evil,
that good may come. The idea is
false and pernicious. Christians always
suffer when they compromise with sin.
They are separated from the world,
and are to win the world to Christ, by
showing that they have something
better than the world has. The common plea, that a strict adherence to
Christian principles will make the
impression that religion is hard and

void of pleasure, and that it is better to join the wicked in their pleasures, so as to have influence over them, is false and deceptive. If it is true of the young, it must also be of the old; and if true of one thing, it must be of another. Instead of gaining power by joining the world, Christians surrender what they have, and are regarded as hypocritical and weak in principle. No one would think of winning others to a proper observance of the Sabbath, by joining them in violating it. No one would think of inducing associates to quit the use of profane language, by occasionally joining them in the use of it. Why then be deceived with the equally absurd idea of winning others from their sinful pleasures, by occasionally meeting them at the theatre, saloon, or card-table? The

Christian has no power but what he gains by standing firmly by his Christian principles. When Christ is forsaken, all power for good over the world is gone. The Saviour said: "Without me ye can do nothing," and his help cannot be secured by forsaking him.

The theatre, dance, cards, and wine-cup, have been mentioned, because they are the chief sources of pleasure to what are called the more respectable or fashionable part of the irreligious community. It is on this account that they become so much more dangerous to church members, than other pleasures not regarded so respectable. One may be a very honorable and moral person, and not be a Christian. Many church members are of this class. Those, however, who would enjoy the higher, purer pleasures of a life in Christ, and have influence to help others to gain it, must avoid the practices which are so purely of the world, and which uniformly destroy the Christian influence of those who indulge in them. Respectable, fashionable people live in sin as truly as those who may not have such high standing in society. Christians, which all church members ought to be, are, by their profession of faith in Christ, separated from the world, and conformity to the world is forbidden in unmistakable terms.

The Christian needs to study carefully this marked difference between the Church and the world, between the lovers of pleasure and the lovers of God. Irreligious persons have no pleasure in the duties of religion, or in communion with God. Hence, all the pleasure they have, or hope for, is in the things of the present time. They have nothing beyond what this present life affords. The greatest joy and comfort of Christians is in the fact that in Christ they have a hope of a better world, and of unending pleasures—pleasures infinitely higher than the pleasures of sin. To get the full benefit of these great truths, and to have the life brought under their influence, they must be well kept in mind. The greater good and purer pleasure which a life in Christ assures, must be weighed in the balance with the short-lived and illusive gratifications of the flesh.

These are things which young Christians have to learn, and many learn slowly. The design of this little book is to help all who read it to avoid the influences which have robbed so many of their usefulness and happiness. All who have started in this course, should "so run that they may obtain." All should make it an invariable rule to be on the side of safety, when there is any danger to Christian character and spiritual comfort. All worldly pleasures combined, are not comparable with those which may be found all along the way of Christian self-denial, and especially at the close, by those who give up the world for Christ, and follow him. "Be not deceived."

THE DOCTRINES.

How precious is the book divine,
  By inspiration given!
Bright as a lamp its doctrines shine,
  To guide our souls to heaven.

O'er all the strait and narrow way
  Its radiant beams are cast;
A light whose never weary ray
  Grows brightest at the last.

It sweetly cheers our drooping hearts,
  In this dark vale of tears;
Life, light, and joy it still imparts,
  And quells our rising fears.

This lamp, through all the tedious night
  Of life shall guide our way,
Till we behold the clearer light
  Of an eternal day.

THE DOCTRINES.

JESUS said: "If any man will do his will, he shall know of the doctrine." Paul, in charging Timothy to preach the word, said: "The time will come when they will not endure sound doctrine; but after their own lusts shall they heap to themselves teachers, having itching ears; and they shall turn away *their* ears from the truth, and shall be turned unto fables." The doctrines of the Cross have always been an offense to the world, and the enemies of the Bible and Christianity cry out against teaching and preaching them. The sentiment is quite common, that it does not make much difference what one believes, provided he is sincere. This is a serious error, for the Saviour says: "Ye shall know the truth, and the truth shall make you free." There is no safety in error, "Because God hath from the beginning chosen you to salvation through sanctification of the Spirit and belief of the truth."

The doctrines of the Bible are, by many, supposed to be so profound and mysterious that only ministers and well educated people can understand them. This is a great mistake, for "All Scripture is given by inspiration of God, and is profitable for doctrine, for reproof, for correction, for instruction in righteousness." It could not be thus if too profound to be understood.

The Bible, above all others, is the book of doctrines; and all who would live the Christian life must give atten-

tion to them. The Bible was not given
to the great and wise, but to the people
of all classes and conditions. The great
majority of the race is in ignorance, and
if the Bible were so hard to understand,
as many seem to think, it could be of
no benefit to them. To show, not only
how important its doctrines are, but also
that they can be comprehended by the
young and unlearned, a few of the more
prominent and important are here given:

OF GOD.

The Bible clearly teaches the doctrine
of one God, not of many gods, as the
heathen imagine. It says: "Hear, O
Israel; the Lord our God is one Lord";
"God is a spirit, and they that worship
him must worship him in spirit and in
truth." This plainly declares the existence of God; that he was not made of

wood or stone, like the gods which the heathen make; that he is a spiritual, intelligent being, to be worshiped in spirit, heart, and mind, "For he that cometh to God must believe that he is, and that he is a rewarder of them that diligently seek him."

THE CREATION.

"In the beginning God created the heaven and the earth." "For by him were all things created, that are in heaven, and that are in earth, . . . all things were created by him and for him." "Through faith we understand that the worlds were framed by the word of God, so that things which are seen were not made of things which do appear." This is the Bible doctrine of the creation of all things, making plain to the commonest mind that God gave them existence, and that they did not create themselves, or come into being by chance.

PROVIDENCE.

Having created the heaven and the earth, and man and animals, the Bible shows that God has a care over them, and upholds "all things by the word of his power." "For the eyes of the Lord run to and fro throughout the whole earth, to show himself strong in the behalf of them whose heart is perfect towards him." "Are not two sparrows sold for a farthing? and one of them shall not fall on the ground without your Father. But the very hairs of your head are all numbered. Fear ye not therefore, ye are of more value than many sparrows." "And we know that all things work together for

good to them that love God." For, "If
God be for us, who can be against us."
This is one of the most precious doc-
trines of the Bible.

SIN AND ITS PUNISHMENT.

"Lo, this only have I found, that God
hath made man upright; but they have
sought out many inventions." "For all
have sinned and come short of the
glory of God." "For out of the heart
proceed evil thoughts, murders, adul-
teries, fornications, thefts, false witness,
blasphemies." This doctrine of sin is a
terrible one, it is true, but it takes no
great learning or ability to know it.
The Bible plainly teaches that sin will
be punished. "Wherefore, as by one
man sin entered into the world, and
death by sin; and so death passed upon
all men, for that all have sinned."

"Cursed is every one that continueth not in all things which are written in the book of the law to do them." "Then shall he say also unto them on the left hand, Depart from me, ye cursed, into everlasting fire, prepared for the devil and his angels." "Who shall be punished with everlasting destruction from the presence of the Lord, and from the glory of his power."

THE ATONEMENT.

Being born in sin, as the Scriptures declare, and exposed to eternal death and misery, all must be deeply interested in knowing whether there is any means of deliverance. This provision for the salvation of sinners, made by the suffering and death of Christ, is called the atonement. The Bible therefore says: "God so loved the world,

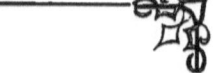

that he gave his only begotten Son,
that whosoever believeth in him should
not perish, but have everlasting life."
"And he is the propitiation for our sins;
and not for ours only, but also for the
sins of the whole world." "And he
said, Go ye into all the world, and
preach the gospel to every creature.
He that believeth and is baptized shall
be saved; but he that believeth not shall
be damned."

REPENTANCE.

Seeing what a terrible thing sin is,
and the great necessity for escaping
from its evils, leads to the doctrine of
repentance—turning from sin to Christ.
The Bible language is: "Let the wicked
forsake his way, and the unrighteous
man his thoughts; and let him return
unto the Lord, and he will have mercy

upon him; and to our God, for he will abundantly pardon." "Repent ye therefore, and be converted; that your sins may be blotted out." "Joy shall be in heaven over one sinner that repenteth."

OF FAITH.

"By grace are ye saved through faith." "Faith cometh by hearing, and hearing by the word of God." "The just shall live by faith." "For we walk by faith, not by sight." "He that believeth on him is not condemned: but he that believeth not is condemned already, because he hath not believed in the name of the only begotten son of God." "Therefore being justified by faith, we have peace with God through our Lord Jesus Christ." "Therefore we conclude that a man is justified by faith without the deeds of the law." "For in Jesus Christ neither circumcision availeth any thing, nor uncircumcision; but faith which worketh by love."

OF REGENERATION.

"A new heart also will I give you, and a new spirit will I put within you." "Jesus answered and said unto him, Verily, verily, I say unto thee, except a man be born again, he cannot see the kingdom of God. Marvel not that I said unto thee, ye must be born again."

LOVE.

"God is love." "For God so loved the world, that he gave his only begotten Son, that whosoever believeth in him should not perish, but have everlasting life." This shows the great interest God felt in man. Such a manifestation of love for sinners claims their love for him in return. "He that loveth not, knoweth not God." "A new commandment I give unto you, That ye also love one another; as I have loved you, that ye also love another." "Let nothing be done through strife or vain glory; but in lowliness of mind, let each esteem other better than themselves." "Therefore all things whatsoever ye would that men should do to you, do ye even so to them."

THE SABBATH.

"And God blessed the seventh day, and sanctified it." "Remember the Sabbath day to keep it holy. Six days shalt thou labor, and do all thy work; but the seventh day is the Sabbath of the Lord thy God; in it thou shalt not do any work; thou, nor thy son, nor thy daughter, thy man-servant, nor thy maid-servant, nor thy cattle."

THE CHURCH.

The Church is made up of all those throughout the world who believe in and serve Christ. These the Scriptures speak of and represent as a human body, with Jesus as the head. "And he is the head of the body, the Church." "And hath put all things under his feet, and gave him to be the head over all things to the Church, which is his body." "For as the body is one, and hath many members, and all the members of that one body, being many, are one body; so also is Christ. For by one Spirit are we all baptized into one body." "Upon this rock I will build my Church, and the gates of hell shall not prevail against it."

OF DEATH.

"Dust thou art, and unto dust shalt thou return." "Whatsoever thy hand findeth to do, do it with thy might; for there is no work, nor device, nor knowledge, nor wisdom in the grave whither thou goest." "Then shall the dust return to the earth as it was; and the spirit shall return unto God who gave it."

THE RESURRECTION.

Although all die and go down into the grave, the Bible teaches the doctrine of a resurrection of the dead. "Marvel not at this; for the hour is coming, in the which all that are in the graves shall hear his voice, and shall come forth, they that have done good unto the resurrection of life; and they that have done evil unto the resurrection of damnation." "For if the dead rise not, then is not Christ raised: and if Christ be not raised, your faith *is* vain; ye are yet in your sins. . . . But now is Christ risen from the dead, *and* become the first-fruits of them that slept. For since by man *came* death, by man *came* also the resurrection of the dead."

THE JUDGMENT.

"He hath appointed a day, in the which he will judge the world in righteousness." "For we must all appear before the judgment seat of Christ; that every one may receive the things *done* in *his* body, according to that he hath done, whether *it be*

good or bad." "And the angels which kept not their first estate, but left their own habitation, he hath reserved in everlasting chains under darkness unto the judgment of the great day."

These are some of the great doctrines of the Bible, set forth by a few brief passages. They need to be studied, for they are essential. Both old and young, learned and ignorant, must know them, and be governed by them in their lives. The fact that they cannot be fully understood in all their bearings does not set aside their claims, or render them unnecessary. Food, as all know, is necessary to the preservation of life, but there is much about what is eaten that the wisest cannot understand or explain. No one understands how the grain grows out of which bread is made; or how, when eaten, it sustains and builds up the body, but all know that bread is necessary, and how to eat it. Clothing, also, is needful, but who knows how the wool, the silk, and the cotton are produced? All, however, know and understand enough of these things to use them and be benefited by them.

It is similar with these great doctrines of the Bible. There may be much connected with them that human wisdom cannot understand, still they are necessary to the salvation and happiness of every one, and enough may be learned to control the life, and lead all who obey them into the ways of pleasantness and the paths of peace. They are not, therefore, to be regarded as the heavy iron yoke which some seem to think them. The language of Jesus is: "Come unto me, all *ye* that labor and are heavy laden, and I will give you rest. Take my yoke upon you, and learn of me; for I am meek and lowly in heart: and ye shall find rest unto your souls. For my yoke *is* easy, and my burden is light."

LIFE IN THE HYMNS.

My song shall be of Jesus,
　When, sitting at his feet,
I call to mind his goodness,
　In meditation sweet;
My song shall be of Jesus,
　Whatever ill betide;
I'll sing the grace that saves me,
　And keeps me at his side.

My song shall be of Jesus,
　While pressing on my way
To reach the blissful region
　Of pure and perfect day.
And when my soul shall enter
　The gate of Eden fair,
A song of praise to Jesus
　I'll sing forever there.

LIFE IN THE HYMNS.

"Singing and making melody in your heart to the Lord."

AMONG the most important helps of the Christian are the hymns of the Church. Very few, however, derive the light, strength, and comfort from the hymns which they might. It is a mistake to conclude that they are of no value unless sung, or only when used in church. They can be read and studied when they cannot be sung.

To illustrate the value of hymns, and the religious sentiment in poetry, this chapter is made up of selections from various sources, giving different phases of Christian life and sentiment. Some of these, and many more just as good, can be found in almost any hymn-book.

Poetry is easily memorized, and it would not require great labor or much time to commit every verse in this book. Those who will carefully study these selections, will see what a rich store of true sentiment they contain. Hymns or verses committed to memory can be sung or repeated any where, and upon any occasion. When but a little boy at school, the writer was required by the "master" to commit as "a task," these stanzas:

> From all that dwell below the skies,
> Let the Creator's praise arise;
> Let the Redeemer's name be sung
> Through every land, by every tongue.
>
> Eternal are thy mercies, Lord;
> Eternal truth attends thy word;
> Thy praise shall sound from shore to shore,
> Till suns shall rise and set no more.

He has never forgotten these words, nor outgrown their influence.

Theodore Monod, an eminent minister in France, wrote the following, which so beautifully shows the different stages of feeling and struggling through which the soul passes in being transformed from the selfish, sinful state, into the image and likeness of Christ:

> O the bitter shame and sorrow
>   That a time could ever be
> When I let the Saviour's pity
> Plead in vain, and proudly answered:
>   "*All of self, and none of Thee!*"
>
> Yet he found me. I beheld him
>   Bleeding on the accursed tree,
> Heard him pray, "Forgive them, Father!"
> And my wistful heart said faintly:
>   "*Some of self, and some of Thee.*"
>
> Day by day his tender mercy,
>   Healing, helping, full, and free,
> Sweet and strong, and ah! so patient,
> Brought me lower, while I whispered:
>   "*Less of self, and more of Thee.*"

Higher than the highest heavens,
　Deeper than the deepest sea,
Lord, thy love at last hath conquered;
Grant me now my soul's desire—
　　"*None of self, and all of Thee.*"

The Christian, wearied with the troubles and anxieties of life, as all sometimes become, cannot fail to gain new strength and courage from Steele's hymn:

Dear refuge of my weary soul,
　On thee, when sorrows rise,
On thee, when waves of trouble roll.
　My fainting hope relies.

To thee I tell each rising grief,
　For thou alone canst heal;
Thy word can bring a sweet relief
　For every pain I feel.

But O! when gloomy doubts prevail,
　I fear to call thee mine;
The springs of comfort seem to fail,
　And all my hopes decline.

Yet, gracious God, where shall I flee?
　Thou art my only trust;

And still my soul would cleave to thee,
　　Though prostrate in the dust.

Thy mercy seat is open still,
　　Here let my soul retreat;
With humble hope attend thy will,
　　And wait beneath thy feet.

A more cheering and inspiriting sentiment runs through this "Song of Hope:"

I hear it singing, singing sweetly,
　　Softly in an undertone,
Singing as if God had taught it,
　　"It is better farther on!"

Night and day it sings the sonnet,
　　Sings it while I sit alone,
Sings it so my heart will hear it,
　　"It is better farther on!"

Sits upon the grave and sings it,
　　Sings it when the heart would groan,
Sings it when the shadows darken,
　　"It is better farther on!"

Farther on! How much farther?
　　Count the mile-stones one by one.
No; no counting—only trusting
　　"It is better farther on!"

What Christ, in various relations, becomes to those who trust him, and the Christian's dependence upon him for help in meeting daily trials and temptations, is shown by Dr. Bonar in the beautiful hymn,

CHRIST MY ALL.

In the hour when guilt assails me,
 And my long, long sins appall,
Then I haste to the Forgiver,—
 On his gracious name I call.
There I find the heavenly fullness,—
 Christ my righteousness, my all!
There I find divine completeness,—
 Christ my cleanser, Christ my all!

In the day when earth attracts me,
 When its pleasures would enthrall,
When its loveliness would blind me,
 And to creature-love recall;
Then I turn to brighter beauty,—
 Christ my glory, and my all!
Then I turn to fairer splendor,—
 Christ my treasure, and my all!

In the night when sorrow clouds me,
 And the burning tear-drops fall,

Then I look for One to wipe them,—
On his changeless name I call.
Then I sing the song of patience,
Christ my brother, and my all!
And I rest upon his bosom,—
Christ my solace, and my all!

In the day when sickness weakens,
And life's solemn shadows fall,
And the deathbed curtains warn me
Of my coming funeral;
Then I think of resurrection,—
Christ my life, my health, my all!
Then I think of incorruption,—
Christ my everlasting all!

In the land of promised glory,
In the day of festival,
Day of marriage and of triumph,
In the angel-crowded hall;
This shall ever be my burden,—
Christ my glory, and my all!
This shall ever be my anthem,—
Christ my bridegroom, and my all!

The difference between what we endure for Christ and what he bore for
us; and also the light, joy, and crown

which the Cross secures to those who bear it, are beautifully outlined by Stockton in

THE HALLOWED CROSS.

The cross! the cross! the blood-stain'd cross!
    The hallow'd cross I see!
Reminding me of precious blood,
    That once was shed for me.

The cross! the cross! that heavy cross,
    My Saviour bore for me,
Which bow'd him to the earth with grief,
    On sad Mount Calvary.

How light! how light! this precious cross,
    Presented to my view;
And while, with care, I take it up,
    Behold the crown my due.

The crown! the crown! the glorious crown!
    The crown of victory!
The crown of life! it shall be mine!
    When I shall Jesus see.

My tears, unbidden, seem to flow
    For love, unbounded love,
Which guides me through this world of woe,
    And points to joys above.

A similar thought runs through Hall's

ALL TO CHRIST I OWE.

I hear the Saviour say,
  Thy strength indeed is small;
Child of weakness, watch and pray,
  Find in me thine all in all

Then down beneath his cross
  I'll lay my sin-sick soul;
For naught have I to bring,
  Thy grace must make me whole.

When from my dying bed
  My ransomed soul shall rise,
Then "Jesus paid it all"
  Shall rend the vaulted skies.

And when before the throne
  I stand in him complete,
I'll lay my trophies down,
  All down at Jesus' feet.

    Jesus paid it all,
      All to him I owe;
    Sin had left a crimson stain;
      He washed it white as snow.

The comfort and repose which faith

inspires, and the consolation that comes from the assurance that Jesus is an ever present Saviour, are strongly impressed by these hymns:

"My times are in thy hand:"
My God! I wish them there;
My life, my friends, my soul, I leave
Entirely to thy care.

"My times are in thy hand,"
Whatever they may be;
Pleasing or painful, dark or bright,
As best may seem to thee.

"My times are in thy hand"—
Why should I doubt or fear?
My Father's hand will never cause
His child a needless tear.

"My times are in thy hand"—
Jesus the crucified!
The hand my cruel sins had pierced,
Is now my guard and guide.

———

Always with us, always with us—
Words of cheer and words of love;
Thus the risen Saviour whispers,
From his dwelling place above.

With us when we toil in sadness,
　Sowing much and reaping none;
Telling us that in the future
　Golden harvests shall be won.

With us when the storm is sweeping
　O'er our pathway dark and drear;
Waking hope within our bosoms,
　Stilling every anxious fear.

With us in the lonely valley,
　When we cross the chilling stream;
Lighting up the steps to glory
　With salvation's radiant beam.

This hymn, by Edgar Page, used by Mr. Sankey, expresses the trust which all should seek to have:

Simply trusting every day,
　Trusting thro' a stormy way;
Even when my faith is small,
　Trusting Jesus, that is all.

Brightly doth his Spirit shine
　Into this poor heart of mine;
While he leads I cannot fall,
　Trusting Jesus, that is all.

Singing, if my way is clear;
　Praying, if the path is drear;

If in danger, for him call;
Trusting Jesus, that is all.

Trusting him while life shall last,
Trusting him till earth is past;
Till within the jasper wall,
Trusting Jesus, that is all.

P. P. Bliss, in the following beautiful little hymn, shows how the Christian's joy grows in the heart, by being repeated in the mind:

Repeat the story o'er and o'er,
Of *grace* so full and free;
I love to hear it more and more,
Since grace has rescued me.

Of *peace* I only knew the name,
Nor found my soul its rest,
Until the sweet-voiced angel came
To soothe my weary breast.

My highest place is lying low
At my Redeemer's feet;
No real *joy* in life I know,
But in his service sweet.

And, oh, what rapture will it be
With all the host above,

To sing through all eternity
The wonders of his *love*.

Dependence upon the Lord for grace
to help and guide in daily duties, is
strongly presented in a hymn by Mrs.
Annie S. Hawes:

> O Lord, 'tis not enough
>   That thou dost point the way,
> But in it thou must plant my feet,
>   And guide me day by day;
> Thy truth doth make it plain,
>   Thro' thy blest Comforter,--
> So very plain that my poor heart
>   May neither doubt nor err.
>
> It is the narrow way,
>   Cast up for all thy saints,
> Which brightens unto perfect day,—
>   And yet my spirit faints;
> So oft I turn aside
>   For some delusive joy,
> Or wander farther still from thee
>   When trifling fears annoy.
>
> Sometimes my doubting soul
>   Turns all her gaze within,

And, thoughtless both of cross and crown,
Falls into some new sin;
'Tis not enough, O Lord,
That thou dost point the way;
I pray thee, plant my feet therein,
And keep them day by day.

Many hymns are prayers and tend to cultivate the spirit of devotion in the minds of those who repeat them and meditate upon them. Only an illustration or two can be given here, but the hymn books abound with them.

Saviour! teach me, day by day,
Love's sweet lesson to obey;
Sweeter lesson cannot be,
Loving him who first loved me.

With a childlike heart of love,
At thy bidding may I move;
Prompt to serve and follow thee,
Loving him who first loved me.

Teach me all' thy steps to trace,
Strong to follow in thy grace;
Learning how to love from thee,
Loving him who first loved me.

LIFE IN THE HYMNS.

Love in loving finds employ—
In obedience all her joy;
Ever new that joy will be,
Loving him who first loved me.

Thus may I rejoice to show
That I feel the love I owe;
Singing, till thy face I see,
Of his love who first loved me.

What a friend we have in Jesus,
  All our sins and griefs to bear;
What a privilege to carry
  Everything to God in prayer.
Oh, what peace we often forfeit,
  Oh, what needless pain we bear—
All because we do not carry
  Everything to God in prayer.

Have we trials and temptations?
  Is there trouble anywhere?
We should never be discouraged,
  Take it to the Lord in prayer.
Can we find a friend so faithful,
  Who will all our sorrows share?
Jesus knows our every weakness,
  Take it to the Lord in prayer.

Are we weak and heavy-laden,
  'Cumbered with a load of care?

Precious Saviour, still our refuge,
  Take it to the Lord in prayer.
Do thy friends despise, forsake thee?
  Take it to the Lord in prayer;
In his arms he'll take and shield thee;
  Thou wilt find a solace there.

As an evening prayer, showing re-
sponsibility for the hours of the day
and their improvement, the following
is good:

My Father! God of life and light,
  Ere evening's hour hath ebb'd away,
Before thy throne of grace to-night
  I offer up this closing day.

Fresh from thy hand, this morn it rose
  Divinely fair, sublimely meet;
I bring it back at evening's close,
  Alas! how changed, how incomplete!

One plea alone my heart can claim
  For such a tribute, soil'd and dim;
I offer it in Jesus' name,
  Make thou its darkness light in him.

I bring thee all this day hath brought,
  Its storms and sunshine, joy and pain;

Its every word and deed and thought;
 Its hope and fear, its loss and gain.

I bring to thee, to purify,
 Its few faint thoughts of thee and heaven;
I bring thee all its tears to dry,
 And all its sins to be forgiven.

And now, O Lord my God, or ere
 This day in sleep forgotten be,
Its dying breath must rise in prayer,
 And bear my latest thought to thee!

On eyes that weep, on hearts that bleed,
 May all thy richest blessings fall;
I ask thy help for all who need,
 And asking this, I pray for all.

Thus, Lord, this night I yield to thee;
 Or if I sleep, or if I wake,
Whate'er I have, whate'er I be,
 Bid me good-night for Jesus' sake.

On a review of a real day's work
for Jesus, nothing could be more ex-
pressive than this hymn. It is especially suitable for ministers, but is
adapted to all true workers. Memorized and repeated or sung, it will

stir and strengthen any heart truly
enlisted in the service of Christ.

One more day's work for Jesus,
One less of life for me!
But heaven is nearer, and Christ is dearer
Than yesterday, to me;
His love and light
Fill all my soul to-night.

One more day's work for Jesus;
How sweet the work has been,
To tell the story, to show the glory,
Where Christ's flock enter in!
How it did shine
In this poor heart of mine!

One more day's work for Jesus—
Oh, yes, a weary day;
But heaven shines clearer, and rest comes nearer,
At each step of the way;
And Christ in all—
Before his face I fall.

Oh, blessed work for Jesus!
Oh, rest at Jesus' feet!
There toil seems pleasure, my wants are treasure,
And pain for him is sweet.
Lord, if I may,
I'll serve another day!

The compass of this little volume will not admit of anything more. Any earnest mind could soon commit all of the selections in this chapter. Those who will do so will be richly rewarded, for they will prove a strength and a delight to all. Looking over them, as was necessary in selecting them, filled our soul with that joy that is inexpressible! Dear Christian reader, will you not study these well, and so enjoy the rich store of truth and sentiment they contain?

ROCK OF AGES.

"Rock of Ages, cleft for me,"
  Thoughtlessly the maiden sung;
Fell the words unconsciously
  From her girlish, guileless tongue.
Sang as little children sing;
  Sang as sing the birds in June;
Fell the words like light leaves down
  On the current of the tune—

LIFE IN THE HYMNS.

"Rock of Ages, cleft for me,
Let me hide myself in thee."

"Let me hide myself in thee."
    Felt her soul no need to hide;
Sweet the song as song could be,
    And she had no thought beside.
All the words unheedingly
    Fell from lips untouched by care,
Dreaming not they each might be
    On some other lips a prayer—
"Rock of Ages, cleft for me,
Let me hide myself in thee."

"Rock of Ages, cleft for me."
    'T was a woman sung them now,
Sung them slow and wearily—
    Wan hand on her aching brow.
Rose the song as storm-tossed bird
    Beats with weary wing the air;
Every note with sorrow stirred,
    Every syllable a prayer—
"Rock of Ages, cleft for me,
Let me hide myself in thee."

"Rock of Ages, cleft for me."
    Lips grown aged sung the hymn,
Trustingly and tenderly;
    Voice grown weak and eyes grown dim.

LIFE IN THE HYMNS.

"Let me hide myself in thee,"
　　Trembling though the voice and low,
Ran the sweet strain peacefully,
　　Like a river in its flow.
Sung as only they can sing
　　Who life's thorny paths have pressed;
Sung as only they can sing
　　Who behold the promised rest;
"Rock of Ages, cleft for me,
Let me hide myself in thee."

"Rock of Ages, cleft for me."
　　Sung above a coffin-lid;
Underneath, all restfully,
　　All life's joys and sorrows hid.
Nevermore, O storm-tossed soul!
　　Nevermore from wind or tide;
Nevermore from billows' roll
　　Wilt thou ever need to hide.
Could the sightless, sunken eyes,
　　Closed beneath the soft gray hair;
Could the mute and stiffened lips,
　　Move again in pleading prayer,
Still, aye still, the words would be,
"Let me hide *myself* in THEE."

PRAISE the God of all creation,
  Praise the Father's boundless love:
Praise the Lamb, our expiation,
  Priest and King enthroned above:
Praise the Fountain of salvation,
  Him by whom our spirits live:
Undivided adoration
  To the one Jehovah give.